Who Will I Be?

A
Halloween
Rebus
Story

By
Shirley Neitzel

Pictures by
Nancy Winslow Parker

Greenwillow
Books

An Imprint of
HarperCollins Publishers

An invitation came for me,

so I'm planning who I'll be

and the costume I'll wear on Halloween.

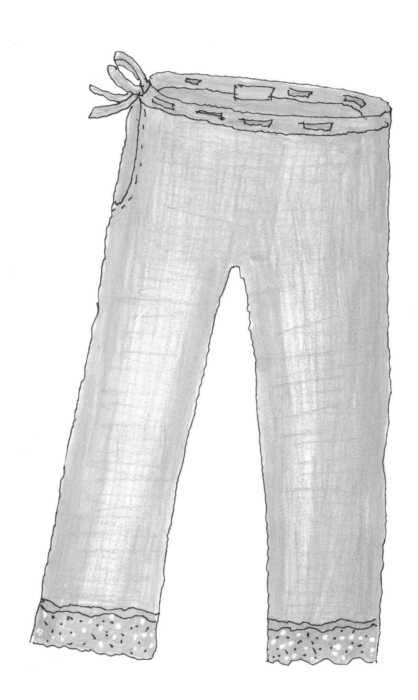

These lace-trimmed pants

just hide my knees

for the costume I'll wear on Halloween.

This silky scarf floats on the breeze,

and lace-trimmed  just hide my knees

for the costume I'll wear on Halloween.

This frilly blouse

has beads of pearl,

my silky 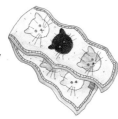 floats on the breeze,

and lace-trimmed  just hide my knees

for the costume I'll wear on Halloween.

This tablecloth

can really swirl,

the frilly  has beads of pearl,

my silky 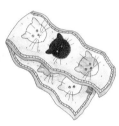 floats on the breeze,

and lace-trimmed  just hide my knees

for the costume I'll wear on Halloween.

These checkered socks

have fringe that swings,

this  can really swirl,

the frilly  has beads of pearl,

my silky  floats on the breeze,

and lace-trimmed  just hide my knees

for the costume I'll wear on Halloween.

My pets will be the purr-fect things

when I wear  with fringe that swings,

the  that I can swirl,

and frilly  with beads of pearl.

My silky  floats on the breeze

and lace-trimmed  just hide my knees

for the costume I'll wear on Halloween.

Who will I be? Have you guessed?

I'll bet you'll know when I get dressed.

I have pantaloons, a ruffled shirt,

fantastic socks, and full-length skirt.

I'll tie a sash around my middle

and hold my lamb that's white and little.

I'll twist foil into a shepherd's crook . . .

and be Bo-peep from the storybook

in the costume I'll wear on Halloween. . . .

Little Bo-peep

Little Bo-peep has lost her sheep,
And doesn't know where to find them.

Or maybe not!

I'll tuck the lace inside my socks

and use the scarf to hide my locks.

I'll cut the foil. I need that shape
to peek out from my shirt and cape.

What do you think of my new look?

I am the pirate Captain Hook!

Ahoy! I'll sail the oceans blue

with Polly and my mateys, too,

in the costume I'll wear on Halloween.

Or maybe not!

For princess Dana and angel Grace
—S. N.

For   Ruby,   Michael,   M. B.,   and Jean   —N. W. P.

Who Will I Be?: A Halloween Rebus Story. Text copyright © 2005 by Shirley Neitzel. Illustrations copyright © 2005 by Nancy Winslow Parker.
All rights reserved. Manufactured in China. www.harperchildrens.com

Watercolor paints, colored pencils, and black pen were used to prepare the full-color art. The text type is Vanquish-Regular.

Library of Congress Cataloging-in-Publication Data
Who will I be?: a Halloween rebus story / by Shirley Neitzel ; pictures by Nancy Winslow Parker.   p.   cm.   "Greenwillow Books."
Summary: When an invitation to a Halloween party arrives, a child gathers supplies to make a costume but cannot decide what to be.
ISBN 0-06-056067-3 (trade). ISBN 0-06-056068-1 (lib. bdg.) (1. Halloween—Fiction. 2. Costume—Fiction. 3. Stories in rhyme.)
I. Parker, Nancy Winslow, ill. II. Title.   PZ8.3.N34Wh 2005   (E)—dc22   2004010867   First Edition   10 9 8 7 6 5 4 3 2 1

Greenwillow Books